ABC

Paddleduck!
#3

Aunt Julie

Order this book online at www.trafford.com
or email orders@trafford.com

Most Trafford titles are also available at major online book retailers.

ISBN: 978-1-4269-9393-0

Trafford rev. 08/31/2011

 www.trafford.com

North America & international
toll-free: 1 888 232 4444 (USA & Canada)
phone: 250 383 6864 ♦ fax: 812 355 4082

Paddleduck # 3

ABC

Aunt Julie

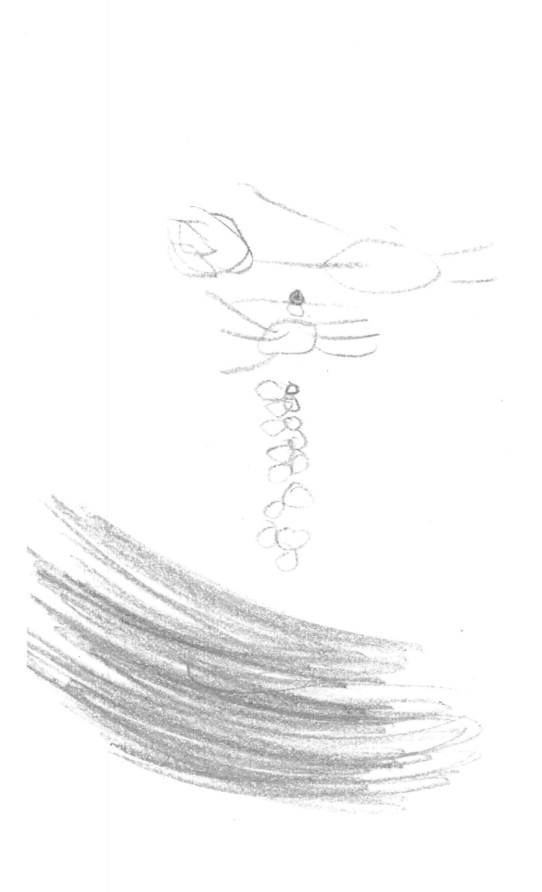

A

ADDISON GAVE AN APPLE TO HER FRIEND AVA THE ALLIGATOR.

ADDISON ἜΔΩΣΕ ἝΝΑ ΜῆΛΟ ΤῆΣ AVA Ο ΦῙΛΟΣ ΤΟΥ ΑΛΙΓΆΤΟΡΑΣ.

ADDISON DIO UNA MANZANA A SU AMIGO AVA LA ALLIGATOR.

ADDISON GAB EINEM APFEL IN IHRER FREUND-AVA DER ALLIGATOR.

ADDISON DIEDE UNA MELA AL SUA AMICO AVA. AVA È UN ALLIGATORE.

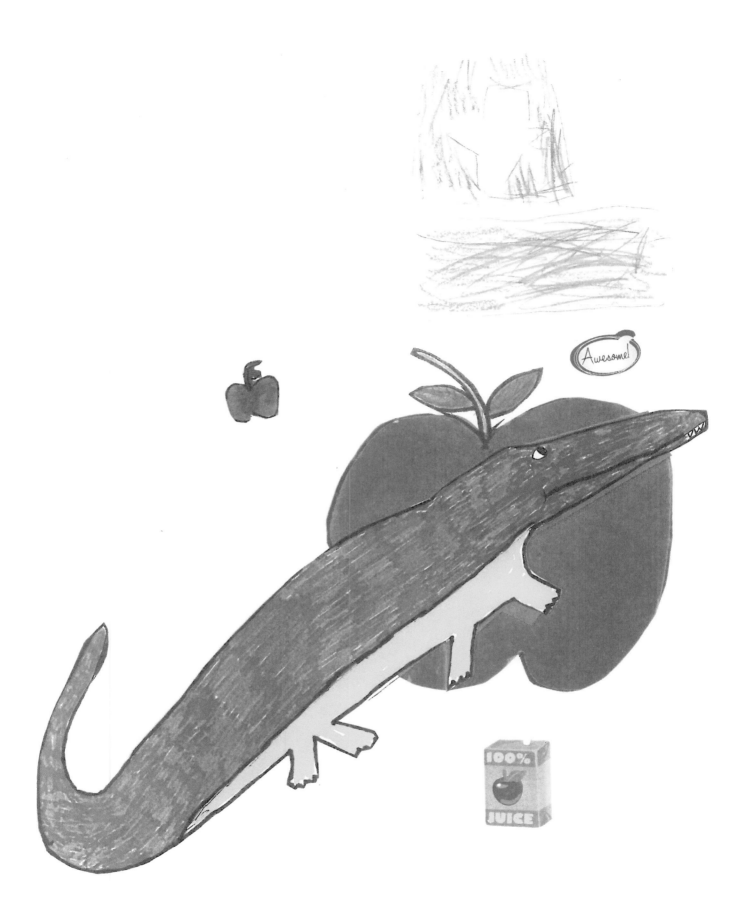

B

BEN HAD A BLUE BOAT. BRODY HOPPED ON THE BOAT. BRODY
IS A BUNNY.

BEN EΊXE ΈNA ΜΠΛΕ ΚΑΡ'ΑΒΙ. ΜΠΡ'ΟΝΤΥ HOPPED ΣΤΟ ΚΑΡ'ΑΒΙ.
ΜΠΡ'ΟΝΤΥ EΊNAI ΈNA BUNNY.

BEN TENÍA UN BARCO AZUL. BRODY SALTARON DEL BARCO.
BRODY ES UN CONEJITO.

BEN HATTE EINE BLAU BOOT. BRODY HÜPFTE AUF DEM BOOT.
BRODY IST EIN HASE.

BEN AVEVA UNA BARCA BLU. BRODY SALTÒ SULLA BARCA. BRODY
È UN CONIGLIETTO.

C

CHRISTIAN IS A COW AND HIS COUSIN CARLA IS A CAT. THEY LIKE TO EAT CARROTS AND CUPCAKES.

CHRISTIAN ΕΊΝΑΙ ΜΙΑ ΑΓΕΛΆΔΑ ΚΑΙ ΤΟΥ CARLA ΞΆΔΕΡΦΟΣ ΕΊΝΑΙ ΜΙΑ ΓΆΤΑ. ΤΟΥΣ ΑΡΈΣΕΙ ΝΑ ΤΡΏΝΕ ΚΑΡΌΤΑ ΚΑΙ CUPCAKES.

CHRISTIAN ES UNA VACA Y SU PRIMO CARLA ES UN GATO. LES GUSTA COMER ZANAHORIAS Y MAGDALENAS.

CHRISTIAN IST EINE KUH UND SEINEM COUSIN-CARLA IST EINE KATZE. SIE GERNE KAROTTEN UND KLEINE KUCHEN ESSEN.

CHRISTIAN È UNA VACCA E SUO CUGINO CARLA È UN GATTO. A LORO PIACE MANGIARE CAROTE E DOLCETTI.

D

DEBBIE IS A DINOSAUR.   DANIELLE HAS DUCK BOOTS.

DEBBIE ΕΊΝΑΙ ΈΝΑΣ ΔΕΙΝΌΣΑΥΡΟΣ. DANIELLE ΈΧΕΙ ΟΙ ΜΠΌΤΕΣ ΠΆΠΙΑ.

DEBBIE ES UN DINOSAURIO. DANIELLE TIENE BOTAS DE PATO.

DEBBIE IST EIN DINOSAURIER.   DANIELLE HAT ENTE STIEFEL.

DEBBIE È CHE UN DINOSAURDANIELLE HA STIVALI DI ANATRA.

E

EASON IS AN ELEPHANT. ELLIS IS HIS GRANDFATHER.

EASON EΊNAI ΈNAΣ EΛΈΦANTAΣ.
ELLIS EΊNAI O ΠAΠΠOΎΣ TOY.

EASON ES UN ELEFANTE.
ELLIS ES SU ABUELO.

EASON IST EIN ELEFANT. SEIN GROßVATER IST.
EASON È UN ELEFANTE. ELLIS È SUO NONNO.

F

MOM LIKES FLOWERS. MOM MET A FROG NAMED FAYE.

ΜΑΜΆ ΑΡΈΣΕΙ ΛΟΥΛΟΎΔΙΑ. ΜΑΜΆ ΣΥΝΆΝΤΗΣΕ ΈΝΑ ΒΆΤΡΑΧΟ
ΠΟΥ ΟΝΟΜΆΖΕΤΑΙ FAYE.

MAMÁ LE GUSTA FLORES. MAMÁ REUNIÓ A UNA RANA LLAMADA A
FAYE.

MOM MAG BLUMEN. MUTTER TRAF EINEN FROSCH NAMENS
FAYE.

EASON È UN ELEFANTE. ELLIS È SUO NONNO.

G

GRAND DADDY LIKES TO EAT GREEN GRAPES. GRAND DADDY
AND JULIE ARE GIRAFFES.

GRAND DADDY ΑΡΈΣΕΙ ΝΑ ΤΡΏΝΕ ΠΡΆΣΙΝΟ ΣΤΑΦΎΛΙΑ. GRAND
DADDY ΚΑΙ JULIE ΕΊΝΑΙ ΚΑΜΗΛΟΠΑΡΔΆΛΕΙΣ.

GRAND DADDY LE GUSTA COMER UVAS VERDES. GRAND DADDY Y
JULIE SON LAS JIRAFAS.

GRAND DADDY GERNE GRÜNE TRAUBEN ZU ESSEN. GRAND
DADDY UND JULIE SIND GIRAFFEN.

GRANDE PAPÀ PIACE MANGIARE UVA VERDE. GRAND DADDY E
JULIE SONO GIRAFFE.

14

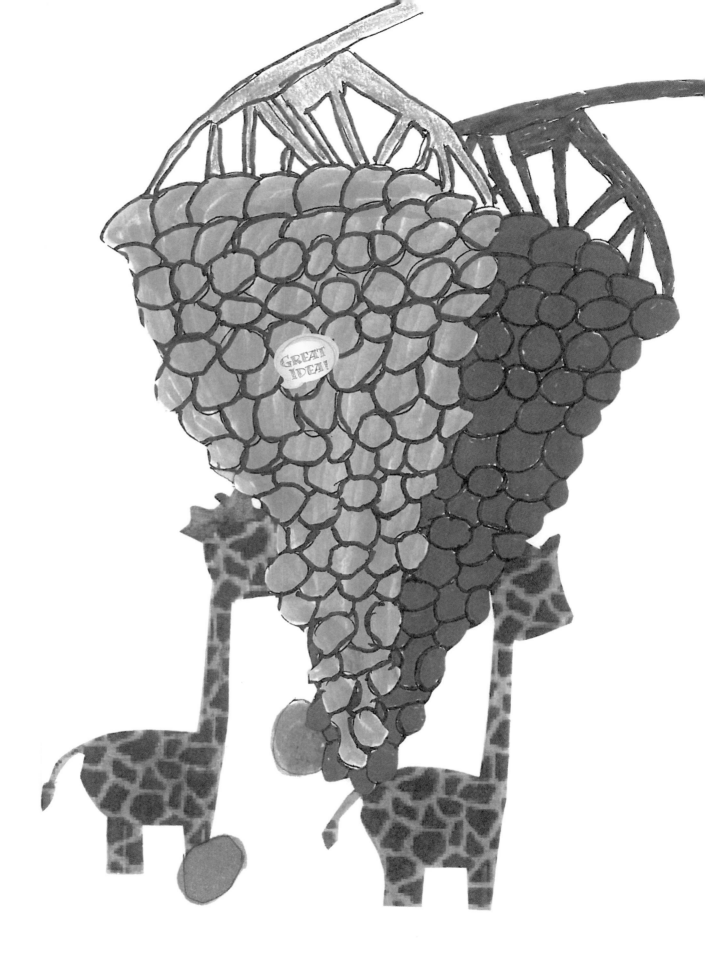

H

HAYLEY LET A HIPPO WEAR HER HAT.

Η ΧΈΙΛΙ ΑΣ ΜΙΑ ΙΠΠΟΠΟΤΑΜΟΣ ΦΘΟΡΆ ΤΗΣ ΚΑΠΈΛΟ.

HAYLEY QUE UN DESGASTE DE HIPONA SU SOMBRERO.

HAYLEY LASSEN EINE HIPPO ABNUTZUNG IHR HAT.

HAYLEY LASCIARE UN'IPPOPOTAMO USURA SUO CAPPELLO.

I

ISAIAH AND IVY WERE FIRST IN LINE FOR ICE CREAM.

ΗΣΑΪΑΣ ΚΑΙ ΙΥΥ ΉΤΑΝ ΠΡΏΤΟ ΣΤΗ ΓΡΑΜΜΉ ΓΙΑ ΤΟ ΠΑΓΩΤΌ.

ISAÍAS Y IVY FUERON PRIMEROS EN LÍNEA DE HELADOS.

JESAJA UND IVY WAREN ERSTER LINIE FÜR EIS.

ISAIA E IVY ERANO IN PRIME LINEA PER IL GELATO.

J

JOSIE AND JESSICA JUMPED IN THE WATER FOR JOSHUA'S JELLY BEANS.

JOSIE KAI JESSICA ΠΉΔΗΞΕ ΣΤΟ ΝΕΡΌ ΓΙΑ ΤΑ ΖΕΛΈ ΦΑΣΌΛΙΑ.

JOSIE Y JESSICA SALTABAN EN EL AGUA PARA JELLY BEANS.

JOSIE UND JESSICA SPRANG IN DAS WASSER FÜR DIE JOSHUA JELLYBEANS.

JOSIE E JESSICA SALTATO IN ACQUA PER JELLY BEAN JOSHUA.

K

KASEN LIKES TO FLY HIS KITE WITH KANDY.

KASEN Θ'ΕΛΕΙ ΝΑ ΠΕΤΟΎΝ ΤΟΥ ΚΙΤΕ ΜΕ KANDY.

KASEN LE GUSTA VOLAR SUS COMETAS CON KANDY.

KASEN GERNE SEINE KITE MIT KANDY FLIEGEN.

KASEN PIACE VOLARE SUO AQUILONE CON KANDY.

L

LISA TOOK LILY FOR A RIDE ON HER BACK. THEY ARE LADY BUGS.

ΛΊΖΑ ΈΛΑΒΕ LILY ΓΙΑ ΜΙΑ ΒΌΛΤΑ ΣΤΙΣ ΠΙΣΩ. ΕΊΝΑΙ LADY ΣΦΆΛΜΑΤΑ.

LISA TOMÓ LILY PARA UN PASEO EN SU ESPALDA. SON MARIQUITAS.

LISA NAHM LILY FÜR EINE FAHRT AUF DEM RÜCKEN. SIE SIND LADY BUGS.

LISA HA PRESO IL GIGLIO PER UN GIRO SULLA SCHIENA. ESSI SONO COCCINELLE.

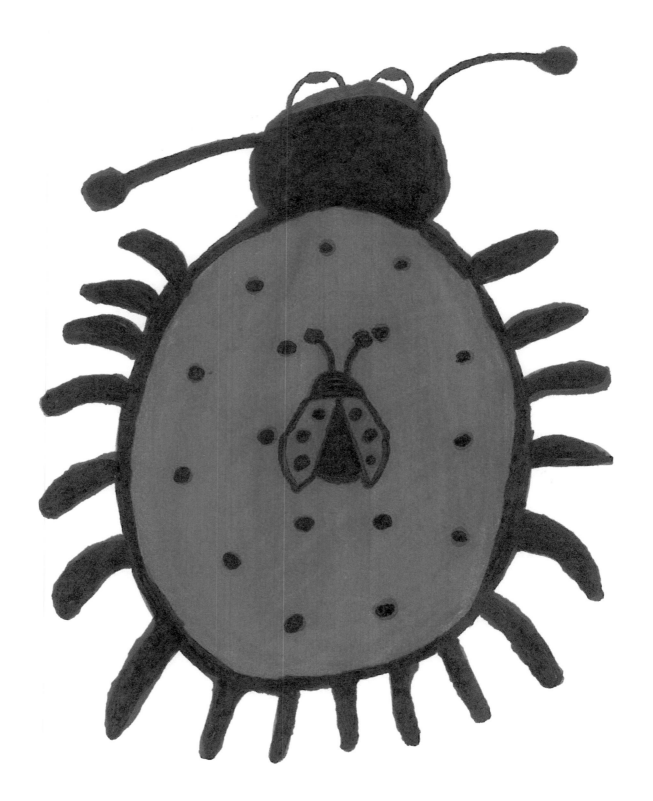

M

MARTHA SAW A MONKEY AND MAMA DELL GAVE HIM A BANANA.

ΜΆΡΘΑ ΕΊΔΕ A MONKEY ΚΑΙ ΤΗΣ ΜΆΜΑ DELL ΈΔΩΣΕ ΤΟΝ A ΜΠΑΝΆΝΑΣ.

MARTHA VIO A MONO Y MAMA DELL DIERON ÉL A BANANA.

MARTHA SAH A MONKEY UND MAMA DELL GAB IHM EINE BANANE.

MARTHA VIDE UNA SCIMMIA E MAMA DELL HA DATO LUI A BANANA.

MAX
THE
MONKEY

N

NANA HEARD NINA THE NIGHTINGALE SINGING NEAR A NEST.

ΝΑΝΆ ΑΚΟΎΣΕΙ ΝΙΝΑ ΣΤΟ ΤΡΑΓΟΎΔΙ ΝΆΙΤΙΝΓΚΕΪΛ ΚΟΝΤΆ ΜΙΑ ΦΩΛΙΆ.

NANA HABÍA ESCUCHADO A NINA EL CANTO DEL RUISEÑOR CERCA DE UN NIDO.

NANA GEHÖRT NINA DEN NACHTIGALL-GESANG IN DER NÄHE EIN NEST.

NANA SENTITO NINA IL CANTO DELL'USIGNOLO NEI PRESSI DI UN NIDO.

O

OLIVER GAVE HIS ORANGE TO AN OCTOPUS.

ΌΛΙΒΕΡ ΈΔΩΣΕ ΤΟΥ ΠΟΡΤΟΚΑΛΊ, ΈΝΑ ΧΤΑΠΌΔΙ.

OLIVER DIO SU NARANJA A UN PULPO.

OLIVER GAB SEINE ORANGE EIN OCTOPUS.

OLIVER HA DATO LA SUA ARANCIONE DI UN POLPO.

P

PATIENCE PICKED PURPLE POPPIES. PETER WAS PLAYING THE PIANO.

ΜΟΒ ΠΑΠΑΡΟΎΝΕΣ ΥΠΟΜΟΝΉ ΠΟΥ ΣΥΛΛΈΧΘΗΚΕ. PETER ΈΠΑΙΖΕ ΠΙΆΝΟ.

PACIENCIA HABÍA ELEGIDO AMAPOLAS PÚRPURAS. PETER ESTABA TOCANDO EL PIANO.

GEDULD NAHM LILA POPPIES. PETER WAR DAS KLAVIER SPIELEN.

PAZIENZA SCELTO VIOLA PAPAVERI. PETER SUONAVA IL PIANOFORTE.

Q

QUINTON HAS A QUILT TO KEEP THE BABY WARM.

QUINTON ΈΧΕΙ ΈΝΑ ΚΑΤΑΣΚΕΥΆΖΟΥΜΕ ΝΑ ΤΗΡΕΊ ΘΕΡΜΟΎ ΤΟ ΜΩΡΌ.

QUINTON TIENE UN TEJIDO PARA MANTENER CALIENTE EL BEBÉ.

QUINTON HAT EINE SAMMELFLÄCHE UM DAS BABY WARM ZU HALTEN.

QUINTON HA UNA TRAPUNTA DI TENERE IL BAMBINO CALDO.

R

REGAN SAW A ROCKET AT THE RODEO.

REGAN ΕΊΔΑ ΈΝΑΝ ΠΥΡΑΥΛΟ ΚΑΤΑ ΤΗΝ RODEO.

REGAN VIO UN COHETE EN EL RODEO.

REGAN SAH EINE RAKETE AUF DIE RODEO.

REGAN VIDE UN RAZZO AL RODEO.

S

STELLA AND SAWYER SAW STARS WHEN THEY WERE EATING STRAWBERRIES.

ΣΤΈΛΛΑ ΚΑΙ ΣΌΓΙΕΡ ΕΊΔΕ ΑΣΤΈΡΙΑ ΌΤΑΝ ΤΡΏΝΕ ΦΡΆΟΥΛΕΣ.

STELLA Y SAWYER VIERON ESTRELLAS CUANDO ELLOS ESTABAN COMIENDO FRESAS.

STELLA UND SAWYER SAH STERNEN BEWERTET, WENN SIE ERDBEEREN ESSEN WAREN.

STELLA E SAWYER VISTO LE STELLE QUANDO ESSI MANGIAVANO LE FRAGOLE.

T

TERRY IS MY DADDY AND TERESA IS A TURTLE IN TEXAS.

TERRY ΕΊΝΑΙ ΜΟΥ DADDY ΚΑΙ TERESA ΕΊΝΑΙ ΜΙΑ ΧΕΛΏΝΑ ΣΤΟ ΤΈΞΑΣ.

TERRY ES MI PAPÁ Y TERESA ES UNA TORTUGA EN TEXAS.

TERRY IST MEIN DADDY UND TERESA IST EINE SCHILDKRÖTE IN TEXAS.

TERRY È MIO PAPÀ E TERESA È UNA TARTARUGA IN TEXAS.

U

UNCLE HAD AN UMBRELLA.

UNCLE EΊΧΕ ΜΙΑ ΟΜΠΡΈΛΛ.

TÍO TENÍA UN PARAGUAS.

UNCLE HATTE EINEN REGENSCHIRM.

ZIO BEN AVEVA UN OMBRELLO.

Ellen

Ryan

V

VICKI IS A VIPOR AND PLAYS A LOVELY VIOLIN.

VICKI ΕΊΝΑΙ ΈΝΑ VIPOR ΚΑΙ ΠΑΊΖΕΙ ΈΝΑ ΥΠΕΡΟΧΟ ΒΙΟΛΊ.

VICKI ES UN VIPOR Y TOCA UN VIOLÍN ENCANTADORA.

VICKI IST EINE VIPOR UND EINE SCHÖNE VIOLINE SPIELT.

VICKI È UN VIPER E SUONA UN VIOLINO BELLO.

WEATHERBY HAS WATERMELON IN HER WAGON.

WEATHERBY ἜΧΕΙ ΚΑΡΠΟΎΖΙ ΤΗΣ ΒΑΓΌΝΙ ΣΙΔΗΡΟΔΡΌΜΟΥ.

WEATHERBY TIENE SANDÍA EN SU CARRO.

WEATHERBY HAT WASSERMELONE IN IHREM WAGEN.

WEATHERBY HA ANGURIA SUL SUO CARRO.

X

XIOALI PLAYED THE XYLOPHONE.

XIOALI ΈΠΑΙΞΕ ΤΟ ΞΥΛΌΟΦΩΝΟ.

XIOLI JUGÓ EL XILÓFONO.

XIOALI SPIELTE DAS XYLOPHON.

XIOALI GIOCATO IL XILOFONO.

XIOALI 玩木琴。

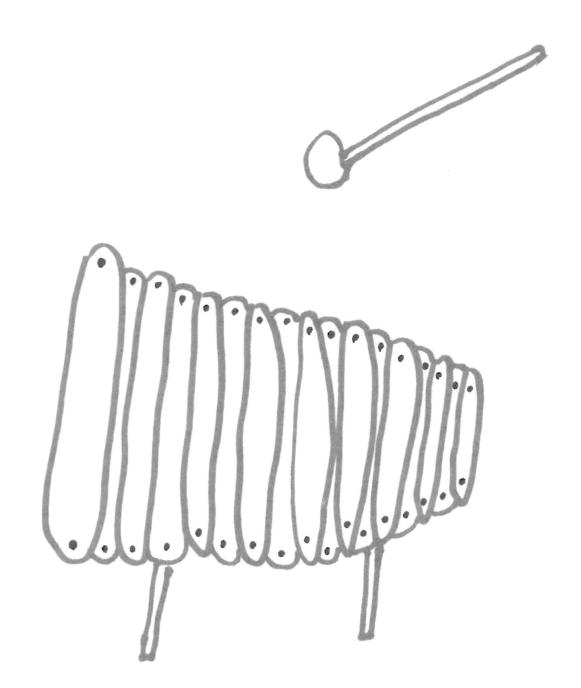

Y

YANNI PLAYED WITH A YELLOW YO-YO.

ΡΏΜΗ ΠΑΊΖΕΤΑΙ ΜΕ ΈΝΑ ΚΊΤΡΙΝΟ YO-YO.

YANNI JUGÓ CON UN YO-YO AMARILLO.

YANNI SPIELTE MIT EIN GELBES JO-JO.

YANNI GIOCATO CON UN GIALLO YO-YO.

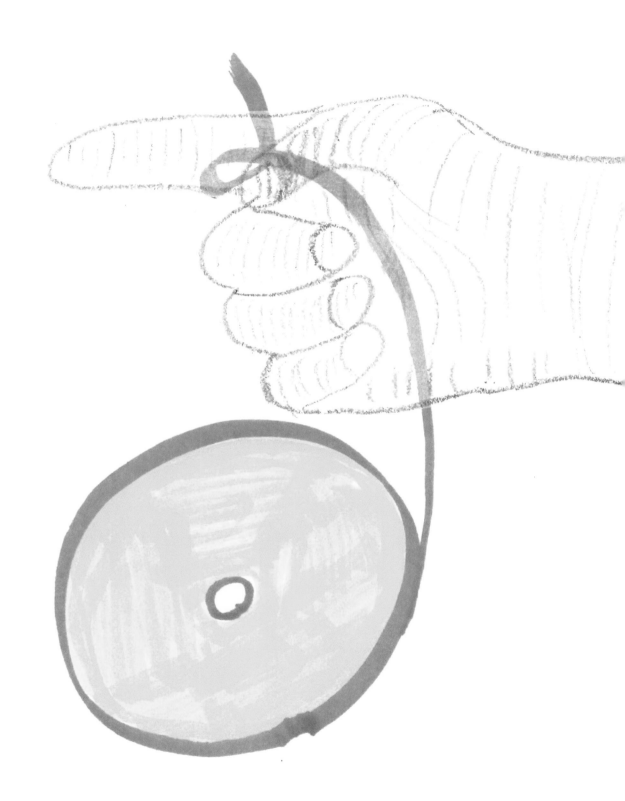

Z

ZACK IS A ZEBRA AT THE ZOO.

ZACK ΕΊΝΑΙ ΈΝΑ ΖΈΒΡΑΣ ΣΕ ΖΩΟΛΟΓΙΚΌ ΚΉΠΟ.

ZACK ES UNA CEBRA EN EL ZOO.

ZACK IST EIN ZEBRA IM ZOO.

ZACK IS A ZEBRA AT THE ZOO.

ZACK È UNA ZEBRA ALLO ZOO.

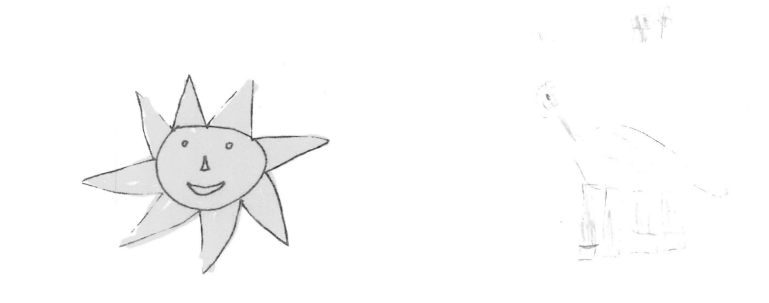

CPSIA information can be obtained
at www.ICGtesting.com
Printed in the USA
247067LV00002B